Murder
in the
Mill

By

John Messingham

To Marie

All the best

Jimmy

Copyright © 2024 John Messingham

All rights reserved.

The characters and events portrayed in this book are fictitious. Any similarity to real persons, living or dead, is coincidental and not intended by the author.

No part of this book may be reproduced, stored in a retrieval system, or transmitted in any form or by any means, electronic, mechanical, photocopying, recording, or otherwise, without the express written permission of the author.

Cover design by John Messingham

Dedication

This book is dedicated to everyone working in and around Waltham Windmill

One

Now that the mornings were lighter and warmer, Adam Black had arrived earlier than usual at the Heritage site where he worked. He had held the site manager position for the last six months after being made redundant from a local accounting firm in Grimsby. The accountancy firm Adam worked for asked the staff to see if anyone would take voluntary redundancy. Adam had already been talking to the board of trustees about taking up the manager's position, so he decided to put his name forward for redundancy.

He drove up the short lane to the site car park, and once out of his car, he walked towards the old railway carriage, where he paused momentarily. The carriage was now empty after the recent fire that had gutted it. Although the ice cream company that had occupied it had renovated it back to its original state, they had now moved into the bigger unit next door. They reopened, to the delight of locals and visitors to the area.

He looked around the grass area between the car park and the main road, and everything looked fine. So, he continued walking through the site, up past a row of small units that housed various businesses and up to the entrance area of the windmill that the site had grown around over the years.

Once he arrived at the base of the windmill, he could see the entrance door was open. He was surprised to see this as the mill was not open today, and he was unaware any maintenance team members were coming in today. He made his way up the small staircase that led to the entrance door, and once he arrived at the door, he pushed it open so he could enter.

Once inside, he looked around but could not see anything unusual. Just as he was going to walk up the staircase to the first floor, he heard footsteps above him. He called out.

"Hello, who is there?"

No answer came back, so he put his shoulder bag on the floor and climbed the stairs. As he began to see the open space of the meal floor in front of him, he could see a dark shadow of what looked like a person standing on the opposite side of the mill from the staircase. Once again, he called out.

"Who's that? What are you doing up here?"

But no sooner had he finished speaking than he noticed the person standing before him was holding a shotgun and pointing it straight at him. He was about to ask who was in front of him again when a loud bang rang out, and a flash of light appeared. All of this happened so suddenly that before he had time to turn and get out of the way, he felt himself pushed back down the stairs by the shot. As he came to rest at the bottom of the stairs, he felt himself drifting away. Before life left his body, he saw the person who had just shot him jump over him and out through the windmill's door, closing it behind them.

This person passing would be the last thing he ever saw, as he was now dead.

Two

The silence of the Heritage site was broken by the sound of police sirens arriving at the entrance and driving up along the lane towards the parking area. Two armed units had been assigned to go to the site and investigate reports of a shot being heard by some of the people living nearby. Both vehicles pulled up in the empty parking area, and all the officers exited and quickly moved to take up positions in preparation for searching the area.

The officers were all too aware that if this was where the shot came from, there might still be someone around who was armed.

The senior officer in charge of both units looked around and then, using his radio, gave his orders.

"Trojan Two, you head up the centre towards the museum entrance and then pass the windmill and back to the old carriage."

Four officers looked towards him as he finished speaking and gave him a thumbs-up signal to confirm they understood the order. They then started to make their way up the centre of the site towards the museum area.

The unit commander then used his radio to inform his team that they would make their way into the parking area behind the rear of the museum and the large shed used by the miniature railway engineers. Within a few seconds, all the officers were going through the site.

*****

June Irwin stood at the kitchen window to the rear of the house she shares with her husband, Tom. The home backs onto the heritage site that is the home of the Waltham Windmill, where June volunteers as a tour guide in the rural life museum. Tom worked as an engineer until his retirement a few years ago. Now, he helps on the miniature railway within the site.

She watched Tom appear in the rear

garden, followed by their dog on its lead. As he opened the rear door, she asked him inquisitively.

"Did you hear that bang? It sounded like a gunshot."

Tom took off his raincoat and shook it a bit out through the door to shake off some of the water droplets that had collected on it during his walk, and as he hung it up near the door, he said.

"No, I didn't hear anything. But then I had my headphones on while I was walking. Mind you, a bloody nutter in a car nearly knocked me over as I was crossing the road."

June looked at him and asked.

"Why did they do that."

Tom replied.

"I don't think it was deliberate, and I didn't recognise the car, but they seemed to be in a bit of a hurry."

Once he had removed his hat and hung it next to his coat, he walked across the kitchen and turned on the kettle.

"Do you want Tea?"

June nodded. Seeing that the dog had wet paws, she picked up a towel near the back door and called the dog over to her. Once the dog was in front of her, she knelt on the floor and dried each paw as Tom made two cups of tea.

She continued speaking while drying the dog's paws.

"Yeah, I'm sure it was a gunshot. I heard a police car passing with its siren going a while after, but I'm unsure where they went. The siren went quiet as they passed."

As Tom finished making the tea, he turned towards her and said.

"Well, I'm sure the boys in blue or black or whatever colour they wear these days will sort out anything that has gone on. Your teas here when you're ready."

June finished drying the dog's paws and got up from the floor.

*****

The armed response unit officers checked doors and windows along their respective routes. All of a sudden, a voice came over the team's radios.

"Trojan One, this is Two."

The Commander grabbed his radio and replied.

"One, go ahead."

"You had better join us at the windmill. We have found something."

The Commander replied to this request.

"OK, I'll head to your location now."

Once the Commander had made his way to the entrance of the windmill, the officer already standing in the doorway said.

"Sir, there's a body at the bottom of the staircase in the mill. It looks like they have a gunshot wound."

The Commander passed the officer in the doorway and looked inside the mill. He looked at the body lying there and then moved back away from the door. The Commander could see two of the other officers had positioned themselves away from the windmill entrance so they could watch out for anyone approaching the mill because there was still a concern that the killer could still be in the area. Looking back at the officer in the doorway, he said.

"You stay here and get the others to maintain their positions."

The officer nodded in agreement, and as the Commander walked away from the windmill, one of his team could be heard over the radio.

"We have finished checking the area to the rear of the museum, and everything is clear."

The Commander pressed the send button on his radio and said.

"Right, OK. You all return to the transport and move down the main road. Put a cordon and checkpoint at the entrance. I'll call in what we have found, so expect a lot of arrivals in the next few minutes."

The voice of his team member replied.

"OK, will do."

*****

Tom and June's attention was drawn to the front of the house as another siren could be heard in the distance. As the sound grew louder, both made their way into the front room and as they stood in the room's large bay window, they watched a police car pass the end of their road. Although the couple could not see the entrance to the heritage site from their front room, the siren silenced quickly after the vehicle had passed their home, leading them to believe the car was making its way to the windmill site.

Tom moved away from June and went back into the kitchen. He said.

"I'd better go and see what is going on. Just in case there's a problem with the railway."

June watched out the window to see if any more cars went by, and as all seemed quiet now, she turned and followed him into the kitchen. As she joined him, Tom said.

"Pour those teas into the travel cups. We'll take them with us."

June moved around the kitchen and grabbed some travel mugs they had used when they went out, putting the two teas Tom had made before into them as they heard the sound of more sirens passing outside. June passed him one of the travel cups, and they headed out of the house, through the rear garden, and out of their garden gate, which led out onto a pathway that allowed them to enter the site near the railway's main shed.

*****

As the sounds of sirens could be heard in the background, Lianne Kinne arrived at the house she shared with her boyfriend, Ben. She had parked the car she was driving in the garage to the side of the house and walked in through the front door. She heard Ben coming in through the back door, so she hurried into the kitchen as he shut the door behind him and said.

"Can you hear those sirens?"

Ben looked back towards the rear door and replied.

"Yeah, they seem to be heading towards the windmill, which is a shame. I was hoping they were coming for you."

Lianne gave Ben a scowling look and said.

"I'll be gone soon enough, don't worry."

They moved to the house's rear door and went into the garden, where they could hear the sirens going silent. Through the bushes and trees to the rear of their house, they could see flashing lights in the heritage site that backed onto their home. Because they were both involved with the site, they became concerned with what might be happening, and as they both looked, Ben said.

"We had better go and see what is going on."

As he spoke, Ben turned back to the door and closed it while Lianne started to walk towards a gap in the bushes at the end of the garden that gave them access to the heritage site. Ben caught up with her, and they both passed through the gap and on a short path that led to the side of the large, corrugated iron shed near the miniature railway.

Three

The site's parking area had become quite full, so a senior officer on site decided that all vehicles arriving at the site should be stopped from entering unless they were required to be near the crime scene, which would mean that everyone except the drivers would have to get out and walk up the lane. The drivers would have to park their vehicles along the main road, walk back, and enter the site on foot.

Because the site was easily accessible through most of its perimeter, many officers had been called to control who entered it without permission. Fortunately, due to the time of day it was, there were quite a few officers available to provide the necessary security, so the site was soon secure with officers positioned all around the site, ready for the expected onlookers who always turned up when a large amount of police activity was taking place anywhere.

As usual, it was not long before the officers sprang into action.

*****

As Ben and Lianne appeared from behind the large shed where the railway staff stored all their trains and equipment, they were spotted by an officer standing at the far end of the main parking area. His position allowed him to see along the parking area between the back of several buildings and the miniature railway line. He nudged one of the other officers standing with him and said.

"We had better go and see what these two want."

They both looked along the parking area towards Ben and Lianne, and as they started to walk towards them, the first officer called out.

"Hey, can you wait there, please?"

Ben and Lianne heard this command but continued walking towards the parking area anyway. As they approached the officers, Ben called ahead to the officers.

"We both work here. We heard all the sirens and wondered what was happening."

The officers walked towards them, and as they all met, the first officer said.

"We'll need you to wait here as there has been an incident near the windmill, and the area has had to be cordoned off to the public."

Ben and Lianne stopped where they were, and the officer took out his notebook, asking as he did.

"Can I get your names and address, please?"

As they gave him their details, he wrote them down in his notebook and asked about their roles on the site and if they had heard anything unusual this morning.

*****

June and Tom Collins walked along the track to the rear of their house towards the site's rear entrance. As they opened and entered the site through the small gate in the fence, they were met by a police officer. June asks.

"What's going on?"

The officer replied.

"There has been an incident up at the windmill."

June looked and, turning towards Tom, said.

"Look, that's Adam's car. He must have got here early this morning."

The officer looked up towards the windmill and then back at June.

"So, you know the person who that car belongs to?"

Tom replied to this question.

"Yes, that's Adam Black's car. He is the manager of the heritage site. We work here as well. June, my wife here, works in the museum, and I work on the trains."

Turning to June, Tom carried on speaking.

"You knew he was coming in early today. He mentioned it yesterday as you, Lianne, and I left for the night."

As they both returned their attention to the officer, the officer took out his notebook and said.

"Right, OK, I can't let you in, but if you can give me your details, I can pass them on to the investigation team. They may want to speak to you at some point."

Once Tom and June had given the officer all their details, June explained that she had heard what she thought was a gunshot while her husband was out walking their dog and that she had been concerned something had happened to him. She explained how relieved she was when he returned to their house with the dog and that they thought they would come along and see what was going on once they heard all the sirens. The officer made a note of everything June told him. Once she had finished, he called the station on his radio. He asked the control room to let whoever would be the senior investigating officer know that he had a couple at the rear gate. They may have helpful information for the investigation.

The control room operator told the officer to bring the couple to the car park and ask them to wait there. He should also keep his notes to hand and pass them on later when an investigating officer is assigned.

Once he had finished his conversation with the control room, he called for another officer to come and take his place so he could do as instructed and escort Tom and June to the car park.

*****

While Tom and June were walking towards the car park with their escort, the officer, now standing at the rear gate, noticed another person walking towards him. As the person arrived, the officer said.

"Can I help you, sir?"

Tom, June and the officer with them heard the talking behind them, so they stopped and turned around. June said.

"Oh, it's him."

The officer looked at June and said.

"Do you know him?"

Tom replied to this question with.

"Yeah, that's Deane Edward's. He's the new housing developer on the old Grimsby Airfield."

The officer sensed tension in Tom's voice, so he quickly asked.

"You don't sound pleased to see him."

Tom said.

"Are you aware of the recent trouble that's been taking place on the site?"

The officer thought for a moment and then remembered there had been some vandalism, break-ins, and even an act of arson in the area over the last few months, he said.

"Do you think he is involved somehow?"

June said.

"I'm sure of it, but you guys have been unable to prove anything."

The officer replied.

"Once I get you down to the car park, I'll get someone to wait with you while I come back and bring him down as well."

Four

DCI Garner and DS Brierton met in the police station's canteen and discussed Brierton's next move as a police officer. She was due to take her Inspectors exam soon, and the station commander, Superintendent Catherine Jones, had called her last night and asked her to pop in and see her. Neither Garner nor Brierton had any idea what the meeting would be about. Still, Jones had always been known as an encouraging commander to the officers under her command. Hence, they both assumed it would be some kind of pep talk.

As they talked and drank, a uniformed officer approached them and sat beside Garner. The officer said.

"Sir, there's been a body found at the Waltham Windmill site, and as you are the next senior investigating officer on the rota, could you attend."

Garner immediately said.

"Yes, OK. I'll head up there now."

The officer got up from the table and left Garner and Brierton alone.

Brierton said.

"Do you want me to cancel my meeting with the Commander?"

To which Garner replied.

"No, you go to your meeting and catch up with me later. I expect the crime scene team will be there for a while."

They both finished their drinks and left the canteen for their office. Once there, they joined Alan Parsons, sitting at his desk reading through emails on his computer.

Parsons looked up from his desk and said.

"Have you heard about the shooting in Waltham?"

Brierton replied to him.

"Yes, looks like we are on the case."

Parsons responded with.

"Right. I'll get ready here then."

Garner collected his jacket and headed out of the office to the heritage site. Brierton sat at her desk as it was just a bit early to go to the Commander's office.

*****

When Garner arrived at the site, he was stopped at the entrance, and as he lowered his window, an officer approached.

"Morning, Sir, it's a bit hectic up there, but I think you'll find a parking space."

Garner replied to the officer.

"OK, thanks. If I cannot get parked, I'll park along the road."

After this brief conversation, the officer returned to the cordon tape across the road and lifted it so Garner could drive underneath it and up to the car park. He was lucky. There were still a few spaces left in the car park, so Garner parked his car and exited it.

He could see a couple of people talking to an officer who was taking notes as they spoke and another couple standing with another officer talking. One last person he noticed was a man standing beside a police car, again talking to an officer who took notes as they spoke. He couldn't be sure, but he thought he recognised the man. It then came to him. It was Deane Edwards, a local developer. Garner recognised him from local newspaper reports. He was the developer building a load of new houses on the old airfield to the back of the heritage site. Garner assumed that was why he was in the area and was now being questioned.

Garner continued looking around and saw one of the station's sergeants standing near the old railway carriage, so he approached him. As he approached the Sergeant, the Sergeant called out.

"DCI Garner. If you come past here, you can go up to the windmill."

*****

Garner quickly realised this would be an excellent opportunity to get one of the mobile police office trucks the station had been loaned into action. The trucks had been loaned to the Grimsby police because the station in Alexandra Road was having a lot of work carried out on it due to its age and the fact it was becoming a bit of a crumbling building. Garner looked around and saw one of the station's sergeants standing nearby, so he walked over to see if he could help get one of the trucks up to the site.

As he approached the Sergeant, Garner said.

"Morning, can you call back to the station and get one of those new mobile offices assigned to us? Can you get it sent up and located in this car park? It may be better than going back and forth to the station."

The Sergeant nodded and said.

"Leave it with me, Sir. I'll get that sorted for you."

Garner smiled and walked away towards the windmill, leaving the Sergeant holding his radio and starting to call back to the station.

Five

"OK, what's happened here then?"

Garner asked as he approached the entrance to the windmill. Standing outside the door talking to one of her colleagues was Rachel Howton, the Crime Scene Manager for this case. She looked up when she heard Garner speak and replied.

"Good morning to you as well."

"Where's your sidekick? Is she not working today? Or has she got fed up with you at last?"

Garner laughed at this and replied.

"No. Brierton's meeting with the Superintendent and discussing her next career move."

Howton smiled and said, using a sarcastic tone.

"So, I was right then. Brierton's had enough of you."

Garner laughed again as he moved past Howton to look inside the mill through the door. As he looked through the door and surveyed the inside, he could see a body lying at the bottom of the wooden staircase leading up to the higher floors, Howton said.

"One male victim, shot at close range with what looks like a shotgun, looking at the mess of him."

Garner looked back and moved out of the doorway towards Howton and asked.

"Any idea of who it is?"

Howton looked at him and said.

"Yeah, he has a driving license in his wallet. The name on it is Adam Black, and the address on the license is local. I have not managed to search the rest of his clothes because of all the blood. I'll see what else he has on him once I get him back to the lab."

Garner nodded and returned to looking

inside the mill. As he did, Howton squeezed past him and returned inside to carry on her scientific examination of the scene. Garner turned away from the door and started to walk back down towards the car park to allow Howton to finish up.

*****

Garner had returned from the windmill where Howton was working and sat on a bench drinking coffee. It was not long before Howton appeared in front of him and said.

"There you are. I have finished my stuff, and the ambulance guys are removing the body and taking it to the morgue. I'll follow them down in a bit."

Garner stood up, saying.

"OK, thanks. Is there anything that stands out that will help us on this one?"

Howton moved around Garner, sat on the bench he had been sitting on, and said.

"I'm saying nothing until I get a hot drink."

As she spoke, one of the officers laughed and said.

"I'll get you one if you want. Tea or Coffee?"

Howton looked at the officer and said.

"It's OK. I have my flask here, so I'll be fine."

She opened one of the large plastic boxes attached to her trolley and pulled out a thermos flask, took the cup from the top and after twisting the top a bit, poured some of the hot contents out and into the cup she had now placed on the table to the side of her and resealing the flask, put it away and took a sip of her drink.

She continued.

"I'll know more once I have carried out the post-mortem, but I can tell you it's a murder because there is no shotgun in the windmill."

Garner looked around, pointed to two officers who were not drinking and said.

"Right, you come with me. I'm on my

own, so you can help me search and see if there is anything there that will get us started."

The officer he had pointed to nodded and started to follow Garner as he walked away from the other officers and back towards the windmill.

*****

As Garner entered the mill, he pulled some rubber gloves from his pocket and put them on his hands. As he looked around the room, he saw a shoulder bag lying on the floor next to the staircase where the body had been found. Garner picked up the bag and opened it. He saw a mobile phone and a thick notebook inside the bag. He took the phone out of the bag and looked at it. The phone was switched off, so Garner pressed a button on the side, and it kicked to life. He could not see any of the phone details as the phone requested a code number to be entered, which means the phone would need an expert to unlock it, which could not be done here. So, Garner took an evidence bag out of his pocket, opened it, and placed the phone into it. He sealed the bag by removing a strip of plastic that concealed a sticky strip across the bag and folding the top over. As usual, he got his glove stuck to the strip and said.

"Bloody bags, they get on my nerves."

Looking at the officers who had accompanied him, who were now trying not to laugh too loud as they thought DCI Garner would not appreciate this, he held out the evidence bag and said sharply.

"Can one of you take this straight back to the station so it can be logged and sent to the wiz kids for analysis?"

One of the officers saw a way to get out of the firing line when Garner got upset about them laughing at him and moved forward, taking the bag from Garner. The officer then quickly escaped the windmill and returned to the parking area to find a car to take him to the station. Garner returned to looking through the bag and removed the notebook he had spotted. There was a big red question mark on the book's cover, so Garner lifted the cover. The first page had what looked like to-do items listed, so Garner put the book back in the bag and kept the bag for further examination once he had finished looking around the mill.

*****

While the investigation was getting started, in and around the windmill where the victim had been found, all of the cars in the parking area were being moved so the mobile office could be driven into the car park and parked opposite the built-up area of the site.

Alan Parsons was travelling in the truck's passenger seat. He had been contacted by the control room to be told the team was getting one of the trucks, and he should gather everything he needed and meet the truck driver outside the station. As the truck came to a standstill, knowing the driver would need a good half hour to prepare the office space in the rear, Parsons got out and asked a uniformed officer if they knew where DCI Garner was. He was told the DCI was in the windmill where the victim had been found, so Parsons went there to meet with Garner.

Once at the windmill entrance, he spoke.

"Hi, we got one of the incident rooms, and it's being prepared as we speak."

Garner turned and looked at Parson's and said.

"Great stuff. I just sent someone back to the station with a mobile phone we found here."

Parsons replied.

"Yeah, he called me before heading to the station to see where I was, so I told him to wait on site until I was ready in the incident room office. I will log the phone along with the other one Rachel Howton sent me."

Garner asked.

"What other phone? The one I sent was found here, inside the mill."

Parsons said.

"Rachel found a mobile in the victim's pocket and sent it over to me to get it sent off for analysis. Maybe he had two phones."

Garner looked around the mill's ground floor to see if he had missed anything, then moved towards the door where Parsons was waiting and said.

"Right, let's look at the office you have for us. We can then have a good look through this bag."

Garner and Parsons left the mill and headed back towards the mobile office in the car park.

Six

DS Rebecca Brierton arrived at the site entrance. Yet, due to the outer cordon and the number of police vehicles lining the lane up to the site, she had to park along the road past the entrance. Brierton left her car and walked back along the road to where several police officers stood guard. As she arrived in front of them, she pulled her ID lanyard out of her jacket and held it up so the officers could read it. One officer recorded her as on-site in the log on his clipboard. The other placed his hand under the police tape stretched across the road and lifted it so she could pass underneath it without getting caught up with it.

Brierton made her way up the lane, and once she saw where the incident room had been parked, she walked to it and entered the room where Parsons sat at a desk.

As she entered the room, he looked up

and across towards Brierton and said.

"Hi there. How did you get on?"

She put her bag down on the desk opposite Parsons and said.

"Fine, I've been put on the list for the next inspector's exam."

Parsons smiled and replied.

"That's great."

While they were talking, the sound of someone coming up the stairs could be heard, followed by someone entering the room and saying something.

"You made it."

Brierton turned to see Garner standing behind her and replied.

"Yes, all is good."

Garner walked over to Parson's desk, placed a notebook before him, and said.

"Can you look through this, please? It was on the victim's desk and looked like it contained details of his plans. Many entries before the latest ones are dated and crossed out, so I am guessing he had dealt with those."

Parsons opened the notebook, and as he flicked through it, he said.

"OK, leave it with me, and I'll look through it and see what I can find."

Garner then headed back towards the door. As he did, he looked at Brierton and said.

"Let's go and see the victim's wife because we need to tell her what has happened and arrange a formal identification."

Brierton nodded, and they both left the trailer. Once outside, Garner looked around and realised he could not get his car out. He turned to Brierton and asked.

"Where's your car?"

She answered.

"Out on the main road, so shall we take mine."

Garner nodded and said.

"OK, that looks like the best idea."

They both made their way across the parking area and back down the lane so they could leave the site.

*****

Once Brierton had started the car and moved forward, she turned around and headed back towards where the victim lived with his wife. As she did, Garner asked.

"How did you get on with the commander?"

Brierton replied.

"Fine, she has put me forward for the next inspector exam in a few months."

Garner thought for a few moments and then replied.

"That's great. We must ensure you have plenty of time to prepare for it."

Brierton continued driving, and within a

few minutes, they were pulling up outside the victim's house. There was already another police car parked just before the house, which surprised them a bit, as usually, it would be the senior investigating officer who spoke to the victim's next of kin first. As they passed the marked police car, they noticed two officers sitting in it. So, when they parked, they both got out and returned to the other vehicle.

As they arrived at the other car, the front doors opened, and two female uniformed officers exited. The driver said.

"Hello, Sir."

Garner and Brierton both looked at the officer, and Brierton said.

"What are you doing here?"

The officer turned towards Brierton and said.

"We were sent down here when there had been a possible identification but told to wait until you arrived and assist as required."

Garner replied.

"Right, that's fine. As you will know, we are sure the victim is Adam Black, so follow us and give us a moment to speak to his wife. We will need to get her down to the morgue as soon as possible so she can formally identify the body, so it might be an idea if you stay with her until then so we can carry on with the investigation."

The officer nodded in agreement, and the two uniformed officers followed as Garner and Brierton walked back to the house and up the garden path to the front door.

Seven

Once they arrived at the house door, Brierton rang the doorbell, and all four waited for an answer. The answer came quite quickly, and as the door opened, a woman appeared in the doorway. Seeing the four officers standing at her front door, she stepped back a bit, asking.

"Hello, how can I help you?"

Brierton took the lead and gently said.

"Hello, are you Mrs Black, Adam Black's wife?"

The woman slowly nodded.

"Yes, is everything alright."

Brierton knew that the quicker they got into the house and got the woman to sit down, the quicker they could move forward with the horrible task of telling her that they believed her husband was dead and had been murdered. So, Brierton led again by showing her warrant card and saying.

"We are police officers. My name is Detective Sergeant Brierton, and this is Detective Chief Inspector Garner. May we come in, please?"

The woman moved back from the door and said."

"You had all better come in."

They all started to enter the house, and she closed the door behind them once they had all passed her. As they all stood in the hallway, she said.

"Please go into the front room."

As she spoke, she pointed to the first door on the right of the hallway, which led into the front sitting room of the house. So, they all headed to that room. Once in the room, Brierton moved to the end of a large sofa and turned to look at the woman standing in the doorway. She then gently said.

"It's Sarah, isn't it?"

To which the woman responded with.

"Yes."

Brierton continued with.

"Please come and sit down."

The woman looked increasingly worried as she followed Brierton's instructions. She moved across the room and sat on the sofa, followed by Brierton, who sat beside her. Brierton looked at the woman and started to speak.

"There has been an incident in the windmill where your husband works, resulting in a fatality."

The woman carried on listening to Brierton, who said.

"I'm sorry to say, but we believe the person who has died is your husband, Adam."

At this point, the woman looked up and around the room at each of the other officers standing around her. Then, she looked back at Brierton, saying,

"Are you sure? He is the site manager. He does not work in the windmill, which I know can be dangerous."

Garner moved forward and replied.

"We are sure it is your husband because he had his driving license in his wallet. Now, is there anyone we can call to come and be with you?"

Sarah replied by just shaking her head and saying.

"Not really. We don't have any close family or friends here."

As she spoke, Garner's mobile phone started to ring, so he left the room to answer the call.

*****

After a few minutes, Garner reappeared in the living room, where Sarah Black and the other officers sat quietly. He signalled Brierton to move over to him. Once she was standing next to him, he said quietly.

"That was a call from Rachel Howton. She is ready for the body to be identified. So, can you take Mrs Black down to the morgue and have a formal identification carried out?"

Brierton looked back towards Sarah Black and answered quietly.

"Right, OK, will do."

Garner walked across, stood before Sarah again, and gently said.

"Sarah, DS Brierton will take you with her so you can confirm it is your husband. These other officers will wait here until you return. I appreciate that this is difficult, but we need you to help us."

Sarah looked up at Garner, then towards Brierton and started to get up from the sofa. As she did, Garner whispered to Brierton.

"I'll head back to the site. Let me know when you have confirmed the identification, and then bring Sarah back here."

Brierton replied.

"OK, I'll get a family liaison officer to meet

me here and join you as soon as possible."

Garner exited the room and entered the hallway, followed by Sarah and Brierton. Everyone except Garner stopped while Sarah grabbed her coat and started to put it on. As he walked down the garden path, Garner left the house and remembered he had come to the house in Brierton's car. But, knowing the site was not that far from the house, he decided to walk back rather than get dropped off.

Eight

Now that the mobile incident room was fully operational, it would be quicker and easier to process all the items showing what was happening in the victim's life, which in turn will hopefully lead to uncovering the person who shot him.

Parsons was now in the process of reading through a notebook that was found in the victim's bag. It was the one with the question mark on the front cover, which intrigued Garner when he saw it. The book did not have a lot of content, but what was present was very interesting. The first couple of pages had a list of financial transactions. All the entries had the same account number and sort code but different values. Parsons knew they would need to find out more about these transactions, so he wrote down the account number and sort code and picked up his phone to call police headquarters, where there is a team that could take the bank account details, contact the relevant bank, and get copies of bank statements for the periods covering the notebook entry dates. After dialling the number, he waited for the call to connect.

*****

Garner had returned from the victim's house and was now back in the site's parking area. He approached the incident room and paused at the bottom of the steps to catch his breath. He looked around the site and saw that apart from some people talking to officers at the inner cordon, things were quieter as most vehicles had left.

Garner turned his attention to the incident room stairs, which he walked up and into the trailer where Parsons was just finishing a telephone call.

*****

As Garner appeared in the room, he said.

"Hello Alan, any news for me."

"Hello, Sir. I've received a message saying the techies have gained access to the mobile phones we sent them and are going through the data now."

Garner sat down at one of the desks in the room and asked.

"What about that notebook?"

Parsons got up, walked around to Garner, and placed the notebook on the desk, opening it as he did. Garner looked at the open book as Parsons said.

"Regarding the financial transactions. I have asked headquarters to get statements and details of the bank where the money was sent from and, if possible, the details of the account the money was sent to. It will take some time, but I thought it might help."

Garner started flicking through the notebook and replied.

"Good work. There must be a reason the victim had this written down."

Then Garner finished flicking through the notebook and stated.

"Becca has taken the victim's wife down to the morgue to identify the body. I'll let you know as soon as it has been confirmed. I'll go and get us some coffee and see if anything else has been found in the area."

Garner closed the notebook and slid it back towards Parsons, who picked it up and as Garner got up from the desk. Parsons returned to his desk, and Garner left the room. But as he did, Parsons called him back into the room.

*****

Garner turned and looked back into the office towards Parsons. Parsons was back at his desk looking at his computer screen and announced.

"I found a photo in the notebook. It was a group of men holding shotguns. It looked like one of them was the victim, so it caught my eye. I sent a copy to the station to the technical team to see if they could identify the people in the picture. I've got an email back with the names of the other people in the photograph holding the shotguns."

Garner came back into the room and joined Parsons at his desk. They both studied the photograph, and then the list of names was added underneath. The list included, as expected, the name of the victim, Adam Black and then three other names. They were Ben Collins and Tom Irwin, and a name Garner had already used today was Deane Edwards. Garner looked at the image for a few more moments and then said.

"I think I have seen all of them today. I think they are outside at this very moment."

Parsons looked at Garner, asking.

"What do you want to do?"

Garner looked at Parsons and said.

"Can you ask around and see if there are some rooms around the site where we can talk to some of the people involved with the site and are hanging around."

Once he had finished speaking, he made his way out of the trailer. He went on with his original plan of getting coffee. He also thought that once they had enough rooms, they could start talking to the people hanging around the site. Especially those who appeared in the photo Parsons had found.

Once Garner had left the incident room, Parsons called one of the sergeants he had seen earlier and asked them to find as many rooms on the site as he could so that they could be used to interview people.

Nine

As Garner walked across the car park, he was met by a group of uniformed officers. The officers had all been speaking to people around the site perimeter and had taken some notes that they thought he would want to know about. So, one of the officers said they had gathered outside the trailer and were about to go in and speak to him when he appeared.

"Sir, we have information we think you should know."

Garner wondered if he was ever going to get a cup of coffee and was going to ask the officers to wait until he got back but decided to speak to them first instead.

"OK, what is it?"

*****

The first officer said.

"I was at the rear gate when Tom and June Irwin arrived. There was another man called Deane Edwards, but someone else spoke to him."

Garner replied.

"OK, I'll speak to them after you've finished. What did the Irwins say?"

The officer started to speak again.

"They said they both work at the Heritage site. June Irwin volunteers at the Rural Life Museum. Apart from hearing the gunshot earlier this morning, she did not have much to say other than that she and her husband headed to the rear of the site when they heard all the police sirens."

Garner chipped in and said.

"Do they know the victim well?"

The officer replied to Garner.

"I get the impression they both knew him quite well because they have been involved with the site for several years."

Garner said.

"OK, sorry to butt in, what about the husband?"

The officer returned to look at his notes and said,

"Looking at the time we think the murder took place, he was out with the family dog. He said he heard nothing because he was wearing headphones and listening to music during the walk. The only thing out of the ordinary he could think of was, when he was crossing the road near his house, a speeding car passed him. But other than that, nothing."

*****

Garner looked around and said.

"Right, who's next?"

The last officer in the group said.

"That'll be me, Sir. I spoke to Lianne Kinne and Ben Collins. They live in Mill Close, which is back on the site. They both said they didn't hear any shooting but heard the sirens as Lianne got home from her morning cleaning job in Holten-le-Clay. So, came out of the back of their house and onto the site."

Garner made more notes in his notebook and then looked back at the officer, who continued.

"Once I had finished speaking to the couple, the man, Ben, walked away, but Lianne didn't straight away. She said we should look closer at the relationship between the victim and June Irwin. She was hinting that something may have been going on between them. But before she said anymore, she looked around and then went to stand near Ben."

Garner wrote some more notes in his notebook and said.

"Anything else?"

The officer looked at his notes and said.

"It may be nothing, but I felt a distance between Lianne and Ben, considering they live together."

Garner replied.

"OK, might be something to bear in mind. Well spotted."

*****

"OK, that's fine. Who spoke to the other chap with the Irwin's?"

Another officer moved forward and said.

"That's me, Sir."

There was a pause in the conversation, Garner said.

"Well, let's hear your notes then."

The officer looked around nervously and said.

"Sorry, yeah, right. The other man was Deane Edwards. I think we all know who he is. I heard June and Tom Irwin comment that he was probably involved in the vandalism and arson that had taken place on the site recently. So, I took him to one side and asked for his details. He didn't want to say anything to me but was keen to get into the site to see what was happening."

Garner looked around at the officers and said.

"I noticed Edwards hanging around. I hear he is trying to buy this site but is not having much luck, so let's keep an open mind on him. If any of you see him leaving, ask him to wait around because I will want to speak to him."

Garner turned his attention back to the officer who had spoken to Edwards and said.

"Don't worry about being nervous. We all had to start at some point. How long have you been with us? And don't look at your watch to work it out."

All the officers started laughing as they all walked away. Even the new guy was relaxed enough to join in the laughter.

*****

As the officers left Garner, his mobile phone rang. He took it out of his pocket and looked at the screen where he saw Brierton's name being displayed. He clicked on the answer button and placed the phone to his ear. The voice at the other end said.

"Hello, Sir. I'm just calling to say that the

victim's wife has formally identified him as Adam Black."

Garner took a moment, although they were reasonably sure who the victim was. It was always a distinct moment in any investigation when the victim or victims were officially known. He replied to the news from Brierton by saying.

"OK, thanks for letting me know. Are you going to head back here now?"

Brierton replied.

"Yes, the thing is, Mrs Black wants to come with me to see if she can help with the investigation in any way. What do you think?"

Garner thought about this for a moment.

"That's fine. Come back here with Mrs Black if you think that's the better option for her. If you bring her back here, get the family liaison officer to meet you and sit them both in the mobile office. We can speak to her first and then others we have identified as worth chatting with. I know this will be hard, but can you try to understand how their marriage was?

There has been a mention of a possible affair between the victim and another woman who works here. I will interview the person who mentioned it as soon as possible."

Brierton replied.

"OK, I'll see what I can find out. Maybe I'll keep Sarah here and ask some questions."

After she finished speaking, Brierton and Garner ended the call on their mobiles. Garner returned to his journey to get coffee for himself and Parsons.

Ten

A uniformed officer appeared at the incident room door. Parsons heard him coming, so he was ready to respond as he appeared in the office doorway. Parsons said.

"Can I help?"

The officer came just inside the doorway and said.

"We have collected all the shotguns owned by Ben Collins and Deane Edwards and sent them to the lab for checking. The only one we cannot get is the one Tom Irwin owns because he said it was stored in a cabinet inside the engineering shed. He says his wife hates having it at the house."

Parsons said.

"What's the problem with getting it?"

The officer replied.

"It looks like it's been stolen from the cabinet where it was being stored. The lock is missing, and the cabinet is empty. We've sealed off the area, and it's being treated as part of the crime scene."

Parsons looked back down at his desk and picked up his mobile phone. As he started to make a call about it, he said,

"OK, I'll let DCI Garner know. Have you called the crime scene guys to come back?"

The officer turned to leave the office but, before leaving, turned back and said.

"Yes, I think they are on the way back now."

Parsons was now waiting for his phone call to Garner to connect, so he gave the officer a thumbs-up signal to confirm he had heard what he said. The officer continued on his way out of the incident room. Once Parson's call connected with Garner, he explained what he had just been told.

Eleven

Garner had managed to get the cups of coffee, and as he walked into the office, Parsons said.

"We have had some rooms made available to us."

As he spoke, he handed Garner a piece of paper with the room details written on it.

Garner looked at the paper, took his notebook out of his pocket, and said.

"OK, cheers. Take Ben Collins to the Gallery at the far end of the courtyard. Lianne Kinne can be taken to the cafe across from there. Split Tom and June Irwin into the two rooms in the empty unit near the car park. When Sarah Black and her liaison officer return, sit them in the old carriage. I want to speak to all the others first and then Sarah Black."

Parsons replied.

"Right, I'll get onto that. Oh, by the way, Becca is on her way back here with Sarah Black. Mrs Black didn't want to stay at the morgue for long once she had identified her husband's body."

Garner replied to this.

"Right, OK. Call Becca back and tell her to take Sarah straight to the carriage."

Garner left the office and went to his car. He had a lot of information running around his head, so he needed a moment to process it all and look at his notes. He would then be ready to speak to everyone who had been identified as maybe having information that would help them narrow down a suspect list and eventually lead to the identity of the killer becoming known.

*****

While Garner was sitting in his car reading his notes, Brierton arrived back at the site and, having spoken to Parsons on the way back, knew to sit Sarah Black in the old railway carriage. The liaison officer had arrived shortly before them and was already in the carriage waiting for them when they arrived. Brierton got Sarah as comfortable as she could and went off to find Garner. As she crossed the parking area towards the incident room, she saw Garner sitting in his car and went over to him.

As she arrived at the car, Garner saw her coming and got out to meet her. He said.

"Hi, how is she holding up?"

Brierton replied.

"As well as can be expected. How have you got on here? Any leads?"

Garner said.

"Not so much leads, but there are a handful of people I think we need to speak to. I have arranged for them to be put into some rooms around the site so we can speak to them further. I'll take the lead as I have been given some notes on what they have said."

"OK, who do you want to start with?"

"Let's start with Lianne Kinne. She has mentioned the possibility of an affair between the victim and another woman who works in the museum. I think we should find out more about this before we speak to the victim's wife about the possibility of her husband being unfaithful."

Twelve

Garner and Brierton had now walked through the site and into the cafe in the far corner of the heritage site. Inside was Lianne Kinne and another officer standing by the door. They both made their way to the table where Lianne sat and sat opposite her. Once settled, Garner spoke.

"Hello, Lianne, isn't it?"

Lianne looked across to Garner and replied.

"Yes. Can I ask why I am here?"

Garner replied.

"Yes, we have asked you to wait here so you can help us understand something you mentioned to another officer earlier today."

Lianne didn't respond to this, so Garner continued.

"I would like to know what makes you think Adam Black and June Irwin were having an affair?"

"Well, it was a bit obvious because they were always sneaking off together during the day, and then there were the two secret mobile phones they used to send messages and speak together."

Garner looked at his notebook and thought that no one else had mentioned any of this, so he knew he would have to speak to everyone else to see if anyone else had suspicions about the relationship between the victim and June Irwin.

"OK, that's all I want to ask for now."

Garner put his notebook into his pocket and got up from the table.

Lianne looked at him and asked.

"Will you be keeping me here much longer?"

Garner replied.

"Just a little longer because we may need to speak to you again."

Thirteen

Garner and Brierton walked out of the cafe building and across the courtyard to the unit used as a gallery. They both entered through the door to see Ben Collins sitting at a small table inside. They sat near him, and Garner pulled some pieces of paper from his folder. Once he had looked at them and through his notebook, he started the interview by saying.

"We have been sent these bank statements that show some large transfers from the Preservation Trust's bank account into your business account.

Garner laid the statements in front of Ben. He looked up and said.

"We are interested in these transfers."

As he spoke, he pointed to the transactions that had been highlighted using a thick yellow highlighter pen. Then he opened the notebook found in Adam's bag at the page that showed the exact amounts of money with question marks next to them. As Ben looked at the statements and then the notebook, he said.

"I'm not sure what you think you have here, but it is nothing suspicious."

Brierton said.

"These amounts add up to almost three hundred thousand pounds, but we cannot find anything to explain why you transferred the funds to your account."

Garner carried on the conversation by saying.

"That kind of money being taken out of an account always makes us suspicious. That is until we have an explanation as to why it was taken. So, if you have an explanation, now would be a good time to tell us."

Ben replied.

"As you may or may not know, Deane Edwards has been trying to get the council to sell him the heritage site for a couple of years now, and the council is coming under increasing pressure to do so."

Ben leaned forward and carried on speaking.

"Adam had devised a plan allowing the trust to purchase the site outright from the council. The money was being transferred to my account so it could be used to pay the advisory and legal costs of the plan without anyone we could not trust finding out until we were ready to approach the council about the plan."

Garner thought about what was being said and asked.

"But why the secrecy?"

Ben replied.

"We have been working with a couple of councillors about this, but Edwards also has friends on the council, and we are worried he will have the plans scuppered if he finds out before we are ready to move."

Brierton said.

"Do you think Edwards has found out about the plan?"

Ben looked at Brierton and said.

"Maybe. If Edwards cannot buy the site and get the access he wants, I know he will lose millions of pounds."

Brierton looked at Garner and said.

"Well, I'm not a builder, so I don't see how he would lose that money without the site."

Both Brierton and Garner looked at Ben and waited for a comment.

"If you look at his plans, he wants to build two developments. One with smaller, cheaper homes that will be accessed via the Louth Road and a separate, more luxurious one on this end could only be accessed through the site. Those houses would be worth a lot less if you could only access them through a large housing estate."

Everyone in the room sat in silence. Garner thought that if Edwards had gotten wind of this plan, the money he could lose could be a real motive to kill Adam, so he asked.

"With Adam out of the way, what would happen to the deal? Surely, you could continue with it even without Adam here."

Ben looked at Garner and replied.

"Not really. You see, Adam was putting up the funds to purchase the site."

Fourteen

Once both Brierton and Garner had entered the room where Tom Irwin was waiting, they sat down. Garner kicked off the interview by asking.

"Right, can you explain why your shotgun is not in your locker? The fact that it was being kept there in the first place, we will deal with later."

Tom replied.

"It was there because June changed her mind about having it in the garage. Which was silly as it was stored in a proper gun cabinet there so would not have been able to be stolen."

Brierton continues with.

"Right, OK, well, come back to that shortly. Can you tell us about your marriage? Are there any problems between you?"

Tom stared at Brierton and then said.

"Everything is fine with us. Thanks very much."

Garner said.

"You are not aware of anything going on between your wife and the victim of the shooting this morning?"

Tom looked towards Garner and said.

"No, everything is fine with us. What are you trying to imply?"

Garner paused for a moment and then carried on speaking.

"We have come across information that suggests your wife, June and Adam were having an affair. So, if you look at this from our point of view, with them being romantically involved behind your back, maybe June was planning to leave you for him. Your shotgun suddenly went missing on the same day Adam was shot dead. How would you like us to view all of this?"

In a raised voice, Tom started to get very angry and said.

"I don't have a clue what you think you know, but none of that crap is true. We are happy, always have been and always will be."

Garner interjected with.

"Right, keep calm, or we won't get anywhere with this."

Tom replied.

"Sorry, but you're talking rubbish."

Brierton said.

"OK, let's return to the shotgun being removed from the garage and stored in the shed. When did June tell you she was unhappy about the gun in the garage?"

Tom had calmed down a bit, so he answered this question in a lower voice.

"Well, that's the funny thing. It had been in the cabinet for years, and June had never had any problems. But I was talking to someone yesterday morning, and they said she had mentioned she was scared of it there and wished I would move it. So, I did."

Brierton said.

"So, it was not June who asked you to move it but someone else?"

Tom said.

"That's right. Lianne told me she had said that to her, so I moved it last night. I was going to tell June that I had moved it, but we had been busy last night, and then all of this happened today, so I have not had a chance to mention it yet."

Fifteen

June was sitting quietly in the other room inside the building near the car park when Brierton opened the door and entered the room. Garner followed straight after, and as they sat down, he said.

"Hello. I just have a couple of quick questions for you."

June looked at Garner and said.

"OK, but I think you are wasting your time as I don't know anything about what happened to Adam."

Garner smiled at June and sat down at the table opposite her.

Garner knew this would be a short interview because all he wanted to do was find out if there was a secret relationship between June and Adam. If there were, this may be a reason to treat June as a suspect, especially if she hoped Adam would leave his wife, but he wouldn't. But if there wasn't anything going on, then the chances are there would be no reason for June to be involved in Adam's death. Of course, if nothing were going on between them, then this would not necessarily clear her husband because just thinking there was an affair could be a motive.

Garner said.

"I'm not going to beat around the bush here. We have information about you and Adam Black being involved in a romantic relationship."

After he had finished speaking, June started to cry. June's crying made Garner think he had hit the nail on the head with his question, so she gave June time to calm down and then said.

"So, does your reaction imply what I said is true?"

June composed herself and replied.

"No, nothing was going on between us. We dated years ago but grew apart. Adam then married Sarah, and shortly after that, I married Tom. We have always been close, but nothing has happened between us since we both got married."

Brierton felt she was telling the truth, and June's reaction was because she was a close friend of Adams. The fact that someone was saying they were having an affair upset her. So, she said.

"OK, but to satisfy us and complete our standard procedures, would you allow us to look through your locker in the museum?"

June looked at Brierton and said.

"Of course you can. I've nothing to hide from you or anyone."

As she spoke, she lifted her handbag onto the table and opened it. Reaching inside, she pulled out a key and passed it across the table to Brierton. Brierton took the keys from her and got up from the table. She started to leave the room, and as she did, she said.

"Thanks. If you can wait here with DCI Garner, I'll get back to you as soon as possible."

*****

Brierton and another officer she had asked to accompany her entered the museum's staff area. It was a small room with a small table, a couple of chairs, and a row of old metal lockers along one wall. Brierton located June's locker and unlocked the padlock on the door using the key June had given her.

Once June's locker was opened, Brierton looked inside while the other officer stood beside her. There was not much in the locker. A pile of reading books took up most of the top shelf, and at the rear of the central area was one of the museum's fleeces, which was hanging on a hook using its hood. She pulled the books out of the cabinet and looked behind them. Nevertheless, there was nothing there, so she passed them to the officer with her, who took the books and started to flick through them one by one to see if anything was hidden within the pages. The officer found nothing within the pages of the books, so they returned them to Brierton, who put them back on the top shelf.

Leaning into the locker, she removed the

jacket from its hook and ran her free hand over it. As she did, she felt something hard in one of the pockets. She could feel a small object inside when she put her hand into the pocket. As she removed the item, she quickly realised it was a mobile phone.

She took an evidence bag from her pocket and placed the phone inside. Then, she hung the jacket back in the locker and locked it up once the door was closed. Both officers then left the museum staff area and returned to the courtyard to return to the interview room.

*****

Brierton re-entered the room where June was still sitting with Garner. She made her way back around the table and sat down once again. Once seated, she placed the evidence bag containing the mobile phone on the table before June and said.

"I just found this in the jacket hanging in your locker."

June picked up the bag and studied the phone inside it. Once she studied closely, she put it back on the table. She looked at Brierton and shook her head, saying.

"That's not mine. I have never seen that phone before."

Brierton picked the phone up from the table and said.

"So, I guess you'll deny knowing the PIN code for the phone then."

June's angrily replied to this.

"Is that a question? I said it's not my phone, so why would I know its PIN code."

Brierton looked momentarily at June and then got up from her chair. As she did, she said.

"That's fine. We will send it to our technical team so the techies can get into it."

June shrugged her shoulders as Brierton got up from her seat and said.

"I'll pop this over to Alan and come straight back."

Garner nodded, and Brierton left the

room, leaving Garner sitting opposite June. They both sat in silence while they waited for Brierton to come back.

*****

Brierton returned to the interview room and sat at the table again. Once she was settled, Garner asked.

"The next thing we want to discuss is your husband's shotgun."

June's said.

"What has his shotgun got to do anything?"

Garner responded.

"We were told you were unhappy with it being stored in your garage."

As Garner finished speaking, he looked directly at June and continued the conversation.

"What did you say to him about it being stored in the garage?"

June looked back at Garner and said.

"I'm not sure what you mean. I have never had a problem with Tom having it in the garage. It was always stored properly and locked in a gun cabinet. I know the cabinet was the right type because I bought it for him when I bought him the shotgun."

Garner was not expecting this because, up until now, he had been under the impression that June hated having the gun at home, but what June was saying now completely contradicted this. He knew he would have to confirm what June said to clarify this misunderstanding, so he asked.

"Do you have the details of when you purchased the cabinet?"

June picked her handbag up again and pulled out her address book. She opened it and laid it on the table for Garner and Brierton to see. Brierton looked at the book and saw the details of a gunsmith in Lincoln, so she took her mobile out of her pocket. After a couple of clicks, Brierton took a photo of the details. Brierton then used her phone to send the image and a message to Parsons, asking him to check June's claim that she had bought the cabinet. She then put her phone down on the table and said.

"Thanks, I've sent that through to someone who can check all of that out for me. It won't take long."

Garner said.

"If the cabinet details check out, you can leave, but it would be helpful if you just went home until we have checked out the phone found in your locker."

Garner looked at Brierton and said.

"Let's go and speak to the other gentleman while Alan checks out the details."

They both got up from their chairs and left the room. Once outside, Garner said.

"If that cabinet stuff checks out, let her and her husband go, but get a couple of officers to sit outside their house. Just to make sure they stay there tonight."

Brierton said.

"OK, I'll arrange that and catch you up."

Sixteen

As Garner entered the old sweet shop unit near the windmill, Deane Edwards looked at him and said.

"At last."

Garner ignored the tone used in the greeting and replied calmly.

"Thank you for waiting around to speak to us. DS Brierton will join us soon, and then we can start."

Edwards glared at Garner and replied sharply.

"Wasn't aware I had much of a choice."

Garner said.

"Well, not really, but looking at your record, I doubt you're that surprised we want to talk to you."

Edwards made a quiet grunt to himself and said.

"Go on then, get on with it."

Garner had guessed he would be met with some attitude from this one. He had looked up his records on the Police computer. Garner was going to make some notes in his notebook. But there were so many complaints against Edwards that Garner had printed the list off instead. Once Garner had sat down, he placed his list in his folder on the table and looked through it. After a while, he looked up at Edwards and said.

"This is quite a list of complaints against you here."

Edwards glared at Garner and replied.

"So, none of them have ever been proved."

Garner returned to looking at the list before him and read some more to himself. Once he had read down most of the page, he said.

"Well, to be fair, you have been convicted

twice for assault, so that's rubbish, isn't it."

Edwards just glared at Garner again and shrugged his shoulders.

Brierton entered the room and sat down next to Garner, who turned the paperwork over and moved his notebook in front of himself, ready to take notes of the conversation he was about to have. He asked.

"The first thing I want to know is where were you this morning?"

Edwards laughed at this question and replied.

"That's easy. I was in the building site office when the shot was fired. I heard it in the distance, and so did the other three guys with me. So that's you stuffed straight away."

What Edwards said was no surprise to Garner as Edwards always had alibis and witnesses to back his stories up. Edwards was one of those guys who could get anyone to say what he wanted because of his reputation as a violent person. So,

Garner decided to leave the interview at this stage and would look to bring Edwards back later either for this investigation or something linked with the comments made by others about his dealings with the council or the recent events within the Heritage site.

So, he just got up from the table and said.

"OK, we must speak to the others to confirm your claim. I guess you will be able to get them to call us."

Once again, Edwards just laughed and said.

"No problem, I'll get them to call as soon as I see them. I guess I can go now?"

Garner nodded and, along with Brierton, left the room.

Seventeen

As they walked down the pathway towards the car park, Garner said.

"You head back to the carriage, and I'll go and get Alan to arrange for them all to be sent home. We'll speak to the wife and then call it a day."

Brierton smiled and carried on walking towards the carriage. As they arrived at the car park, they split up. Brierton went up the stairs to the entrance door of the carriage. Garner walked across the car park to the incident room to arrange for everyone to be allowed to leave and ensure there would be officers sitting outside their houses to ensure they didn't disappear until all their stories had been checked out.

*****

Brierton opened the carriage door and walked in, followed by Garner, who closed the door behind him. As they were sitting down, Brierton said.

"Mrs Black, I'm so sorry to have kept you waiting, but quite a lot is happening."

Sarah Black smiled and said.

"That's OK. I understand you are busy."

As she spoke, she looked at the officer sitting beside her and carried on by saying.

"This lovely officer has been looking after me."

Garner was now sitting at the table and placed his notebook on it, open at the page where he had made notes about what the other officers had told him. He looked up at Sarah and said.

"Right, there's no easy way of asking this, so I will just come out with it and ask."

Sarah looked back across the table towards him with a slightly startled look as he started to speak again.

"We have been told that Adam may have

been romantically involved with another woman who works here at the site."

Sarah looked at Garner and, with a slight chuckle in her voice, said.

"Who told you that?"

Garner responded with.

"I can't tell you that, I'm afraid."

Sarah looked around at Brierton and then back towards Garner.

"Well, whoever told you that is mistaken. We have been married a long time now, and neither of us has been unfaithful."

Garner replied.

"You seem very sure of that."

Sarah said.

"I am. We have been together a long time now, and I think I would know if something was going on behind my back."

She paused for a moment and then said.

"If it was one of the girls in the museum who told you he was having an affair, then they are either lying or just mistaken. You see, Adam and June dated for a couple of years before we got married, and before that, he went out with Lianne a few times, but she was a bit, well, let's just say, intense."

Brierton looked across the table towards Sarah and asked.

"What do you mean by intense?"

Sarah looked back at Brierton and said.

"Adam said she was one of those people who wanted to know everything he did when they weren't together, and when he told her he was finishing with her, she erupted in a right rage and made all kinds of threats. I remember Adam saying that he was worried for a while that she might do something to hurt him. We were quite surprised when she and Ben got together earlier this year, although from what I hear, that is not working out either."

Garner was flicking back through his notebook to an earlier page and, after reading for a moment, said.

"So, are you saying Lianne and Ben have only been together briefly?"

Sarah replied to this with.

"Yes, Ben only moved to his new house, which is back on the site at the end of last year. That's when Lianne seemed to become interested in him. As I said, I'm surprised they have lasted this long as all her past relationships have been very short-lived."

Garner said.

"OK, we'll leave that for now and talk about the site ownership."

Garner looked at Brierton and said.

"Do you want to ask about this one?"

Brierton nodded in agreement and said.

"Are you aware that your husband was putting up the money for the site to be purchased by the preservation trust?"

Sarah responded.

"Yes, I don't know the full details as some

of it was hush-hush. I know that some of the trust members, Ben Collins and Adam, were planning to buy the site to stop Edwards from getting it and ruining it."

Brierton looked at Garner, who said.

"Right, I think that clears that one up for us then. We'll get someone to take you home now. We are going to make further enquiries into some other information we have. If it is OK with you, we will update you in the morning with any developments we make overnight."

Sarah Black smiled at Garner and said.

"OK, thank you for doing your best to sort it all out. Will the liaison officer stay with me tonight?"

Brierton said.

"Yes, if that's what you want. Are you sure there is no one else we can call?"

Sarah shook her head and got out of her chair, so the others got up and exited the carriage.

Eighteen

As Garner pulled into the car park, he saw Brierton standing outside the incident room entrance. He parked up and walked over to her. As he got there, she said.

"Morning, Sir, I've got you a coffee."

Handing him a cup, she turned and entered the incident room, where Alan Parsons was sitting at the middle table. Garner followed her in, and they both sat at the table.

Parsons started by saying.

"I followed up on the money being transferred into Ben Collin's business account by talking to the chairman of the preservation trust, and he confirmed what both Ben and Sarah Black told us."

Garner looked at Parsons and said.

"Right, so we can discount that as a

motive."

Brierton said.

"Looks like it."

*****

Parsons slid the piece of paper with all the details about the money and site purchase to one side, reached behind, and grabbed a computer keyboard from the worktop that ran down the side of the room. He placed it on the table in front of himself. He said.

"I spent some time looking through various CCTV clips last night and think I might have found something interesting."

As he spoke, he pressed a couple of buttons on the keyboard, and everyone's attention switched to a large screen on the room's rear wall.

"I have been through some of the doorbell camera footage the house-to-house team obtained yesterday."

The video on the screen showed a camera view from a large public house near the end of the road leading down towards Waltham. As they watched, they saw a car in the distance turn off the Louth Road and head down towards Waltham. Parsons stopped the video at this point and started to play another clip from a house near the other end of the road.

He started to play the second video on the screen, and as they all watched, they saw the car pull up at the roadside in front of a house just past the entrance to a track leading between two houses. The video showed someone wearing a grey jacket with a hood over their head getting out of the car and walking back towards the track. Parsons paused the video at this point and said.

"If I fast forward this video, you will see the person return to the car and drive off."

Parsons did as he said he would and fast-forwarded the video to the point where what appeared to be the same person walked back to the car, got in and drove off. Parsons stopped the video and said.

"If you look at the time stamp of the car pulling up and then driving off, you'll see it covers the period we think Adam Black was shot."

Garner said.

"Well done, Alan, that's splendid work as usual. Do we know where they went after driving away?"

Alan replied.

"There are some other doorbell cameras further down the road, but none of them show the car passing, so it looks like it turned off before the end of the main road into Waltham.

Garner took his notebook out of his pocket and opened it. He read through his notes for a while and then said.

"We need to speak to Tom Irwin again. He said a car nearly knocked him over when crossing the road with his dog."

Looking at Brierton, he continued with.

"Get an image extracted from that video showing the car and pop round to the Irwins to see if that could be the car he saw."

Parsons chipped in at this point and said.

"I'll print an image of now."

As Parsons printed the image for Brierton, a ping came from the computer he was using. So, as soon as the image finished printing, he handed it to Brierton, who took it and left the office so she could visit Tom Irwin to see if it triggered any more memories about the car that nearly knocked him over. He then looked at the emails on the computer and saw a new one had arrived.

*****

The new email was the report about the mobile phones in the victim's bag and June Irwin's locker. He opened the attachment and started reading it. It showed that the phones had been activated about a year before on the same day. Call logs showed that the two phones were only ever used to contact each other and that calls between them were always answered. The text messages between the devices were similar. Any messages sent between the phones were always responded to quite quickly.

Because none of the calls went unanswered, the report could not provide any transcriptions or sound files of messages left. The text messages mostly contained arrangements of meetings between the two users, with the occasional reference to sexual encounters and flirtatious intentions for future meetings.

One thing that caught Alan's attention was that although no records were found of voicemail messages being left, the answer services on both phones were switched on. He thought this was a bit weird because it would indicate that both phone users knew when the other would call or could always answer the calls when they were made.

Parsons called over to Garner.

"I think you had better see this."

Garner walked over to Alan, stood beside him and said.

"What's up?"

Alan replied.

"I've been through this report about the two phones, and something is a bit odd."

As he spoke, Alan pointed to the last bit of the report. Garner leaned down and started to read the report that Alan was pointing to.

"Because the location details recorded for the phones when they were both powered on show them to be close together, we would consider this to show that both devices were in the same location or very close to each other when used."

Garner stood up and said.

"That's odd, although it does fit with the doubt about something between Adam Black and June Irwin."

Garner started to walk away from Parsons and said.

"Check the location of their main phones and see if the location data matches the two secret phones when switched on. However, I guess it's possible that they only used the phones when they were on site. Still, check anyway."

Alan nodded but replied.

"I'll check, but the times of the calls mean they would spend most of their lives here at the site."

Garner replied.

"Which would probably negate the need for the phones at all. Check anyway so we can be sure of all the data."

*****

While Garner and Parsons waited for the technical team to get back to them with the location details of Adam and June's primary mobile phones, Garner's phone rang. It was Brierton calling him from the Irwin's house. Garner answered the call and said.

"Hi, any news?"

He listened for a few seconds and then said.

"Right, thanks for that. Wait there for now."

He ended the call, turning to Parsons and

said.

"That's the car confirmed as the one that Tom Irwin saw."

Parsons was just about to respond to Garner when his phone rang. So, he answered it and listened for a few seconds before saying.

"Cheers for that. I'll tell DCI Garner straight away."

Garner watched as Parsons ended the call and then waited to hear what he had to say. Parsons looked at Garner and said.

"That was the techs. They checked the location details of the main phones to see if there was any link to the locations of the other two phones we found. They don't match."

Garner was just about to express his disappointment at hearing this when Parsons carried on speaking.

"The thing is. The technical team also checked the location details against the phones against the ones used by the other people you spoke to, and they found a link with one of them."

"Whose is it that links?"

"Lianne Kinne's phone location seems to match."

Garner grabbed his phone to call Brierton, and once she answered, he said.

"Can you meet me at Lianne Kinne's house as soon as possible?"

As he was leaving the office, Garner said.

"Get everyone available to head to her house and secure it. I'll head round now and meet Becca there."

Nineteen

As Brierton arrived at Lianne and Ben's house, she could see them arguing on the front doorstep with another older man. She pulled up and exited her car. As she walked past the patrol car parked outside the house, the two patrol officers exited and followed Brierton up the pathway to where the three people were shouting at each other. As they approached, Lianne could be heard screaming.

"It's none of your business what I do with my life."

Ben shouted back at her.

"That's true, so why are you still here."

The third man standing near Lianne turned and saw Brierton and the two police officers approaching and said.

"Look, now someone's called the police because of your shouting and balling."

As Lianne turned and looked at Brierton, she shouted out.

"No."

As she did, she started running off across the grass in front of the house to escape. But, the two officers who had arrived with Brierton quickly responded and grabbed her as she tried to run. Keeping hold of her, they brought her back to the front door area. Brierton looked at her and asked.

"What's going on here?"

When Ben responded to her question, Brierton's attention was drawn back to Ben and the other man.

"This is Lianne's dad. He has come to take her to his house because she has done my head in. She says she is leaving me, which is fine with me, but Lianne also claims to be still in love with Adam, and if she cannot have him, then no one will."

Brierton looked at Lianne and said.

"Was it you? Was it you who killed Adam?"

While Brierton waited for an answer, she realised Garner and some other officers were rushing to the scene. Garner pointed to Lianne and said.

"Get her into one of the cars and start searching the house."

The two officers holding onto Lianne led her away to one of the cars, and once they had placed handcuffs on her, they sat her in the back of the car, closing the door behind her.

*****

Garner and Brierton waited outside the house as some officers entered. Within a few minutes, the garage door opened. An officer appeared from inside and called out.

"Sir, we've got something here."

Garner and Brierton both walked over to the garage door and went inside. Once there, they were shown a small holdall that contained a grey hoodie covered in blood and a sawn-off shotgun with the initials TI engraved on the stock. Another officer at the back of the garage called over, and when everyone looked towards the officer, they could see them holding up what looked like the shotgun barrels that had been removed from the weapon to make it easier to conceal inside her clothes.

Garner looked at the officer and said.

"Great work. Call the crime scene guys down and let them get to work."

Brierton said.

"Who's car is this then? Why did Tom Irwin recognise it if it is Lianne's?"

A voice came from behind them.

"It's mine. I only let Lianne use it occasionally because of the way she drives."

Brierton turned round to see that it was Lianne's dad speaking, and what he had said explained why Tom had not recognised the car.

As they approached the patrol car where Lianne was sitting, Garner looked at Brierton and said.

"Once we have sorted all this out back at the station. You had better get off and start revising for your exam. I don't want to get the blame for you not passing."

About the Author

John Messingham was born in Hampton, Middlesex, England. After finishing school, he joined the British Army and served as an Infantryman and later trained as a radio operator within the battalion mortar platoon. After his time in the army, he trained as a computer programmer and started a long career in IT. The fiction he writes sometimes draws on both his military and IT backgrounds.

For more information about John and his writing, please visit.

http://johnmessingham.co.uk

By John Messingham

DCI Garner and DS Brierton Murder Mysteries

Series One
The Pier
The Body in the Van
Murder in the Park

Series Two
Murder in the Mill

DCI Garner and DS Brierton Short Stories
Murder on the Mince Pie Special

Printed in Great Britain
by Amazon